CERTIFICATE OF REGISTRATION

This book belongs to

____

ALSO BY BILLY STEERS

Tractor Mac Arrives at the Farm

Tractor Mac You're a Winner

Tractor Mac Harvest Time

Tractor Mac Parade's Best

Tractor Mac Farmers' Market

Tractor Mac Family Reunion

Tractor Mac New Friend

Tractor Mac Friends on the Farm

Tractor Mac Builds a Barn

Tractor Mac Tune-Up

Tractor Mac Saves Christmas

Written and illustrated by

BILLY STEERS

FARRAR STRAUS GIROUX • NEW YORK

TRACTOR MAC AND SIBLEY THE HORSE lived on Stony Meadow Farm. They shared the work and often shared their thoughts.

CIRCUS
SIB

"Do you ever wish you were doing something different, Mac?" asked Sibley one afternoon. "Sometimes I think it would be fun to pull a circus wagon in a parade or maybe a trolley car full of people."

"I am happy being myself," answered the big red tractor. "Why would I want to be something I'm not?"

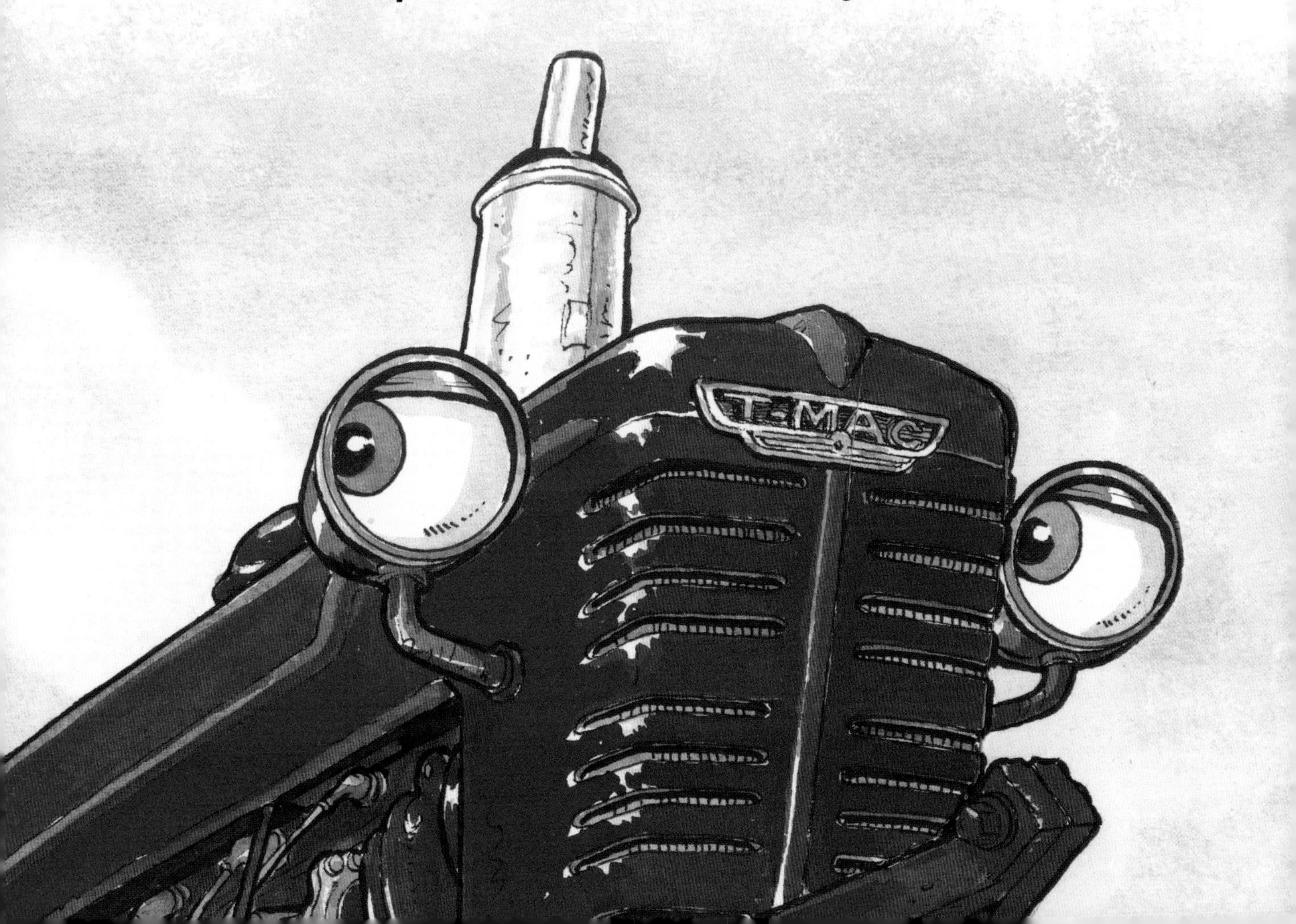

Just then, the two friends heard a sound that was quite different from Mac's normal chugging and popping. It roared overhead as it came near.

"Clear the runway!" a bright yellow airplane shouted as it circled low over their heads.

Tractor Mac stared as the plane bounded to a dusty stop in the hayfield. He had never seen such a beautiful machine.

Smiling passengers climbed out while others stood in line to get on board.

Mac's heart fluttered with excitement. "That plane gives hayrides in the sky!"

Mac wheeled over to the plane.
"What's your name?" he asked.
"My name is Plane Jane,"
said the yellow plane.

"It must be wonderful to fly with the birds! Do you think I could do that?" asked Mac.

"No, you couldn't," she answered. "You don't have any wings, so how could you fly? Ta ta. Off I go into the wild blue."

For the rest of the day, all Mac could think about was flying. What a thrill it must be!

That night, Mac told his story of the bright yellow plane to the birds on the farm. Mac asked them a lot of questions about flying. They talked until late into the night.

Day after day, Mac looked at Plane Jane as she flew overhead with a new load of thrill seekers. Soaring, gliding, looping, rolling.

As Mac watched, he longed more than ever to fly.

SKY RIDES

Then one day, quite by accident, Mac's big chance came. As he was chugging down the hill from the pumpkin patch, something snapped.

SNORT! *PING!*

His brakes stopped working. The heavy load pushed Mac faster and faster. He was rolling down the hill out of control!

He could not stop! *ZOOOOM!*

Suddenly, Mac was flying . . .

. . . for a little while. **SPLOOSH!**

Mac plunged into the pond.

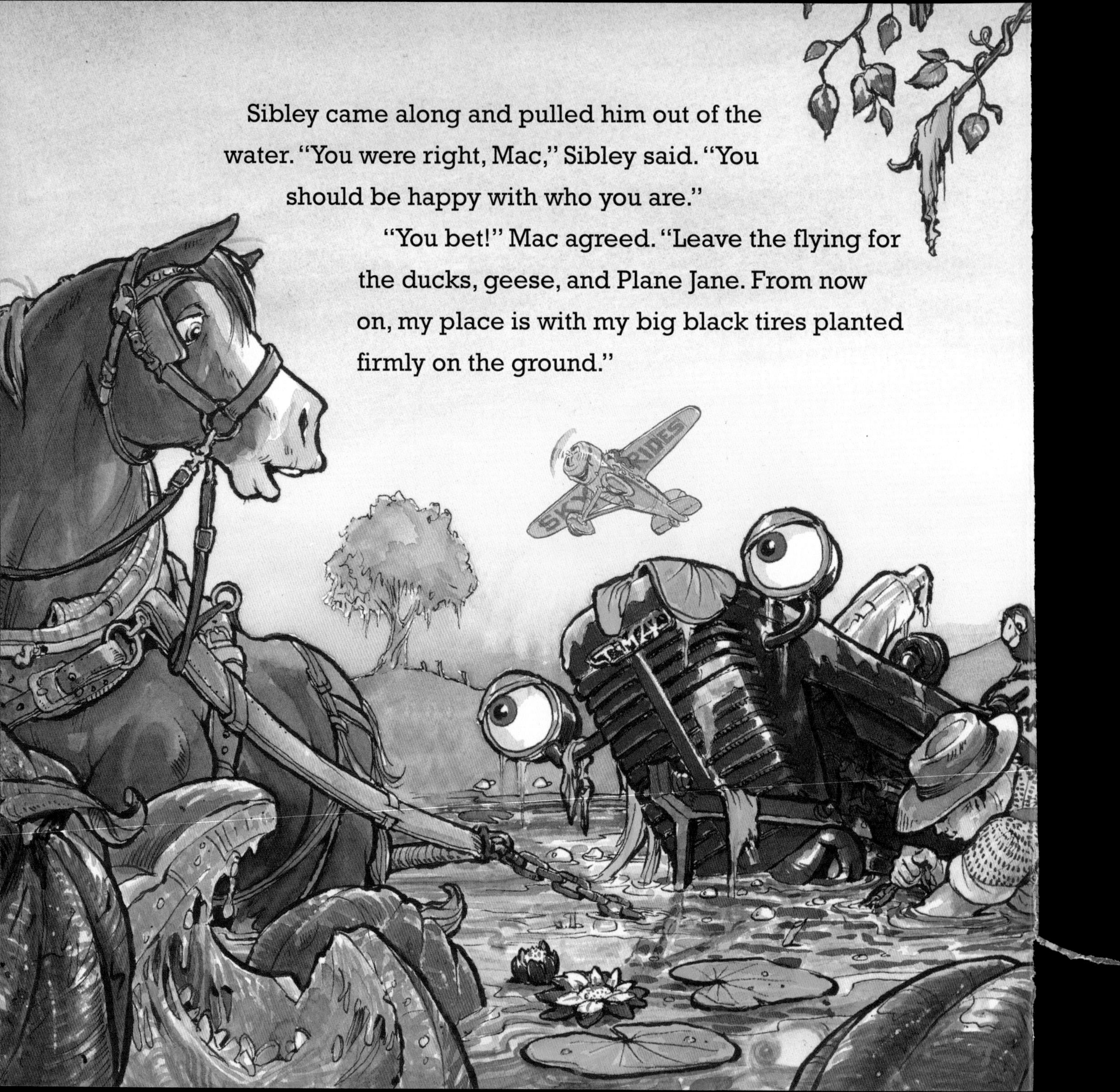

Sibley came along and pulled him out of the water. "You were right, Mac," Sibley said. "You should be happy with who you are."

"You bet!" Mac agreed. "Leave the flying for the ducks, geese, and Plane Jane. From now on, my place is with my big black tires planted firmly on the ground."

To Mom and Dad, who instilled in me the love to both draw and fly

Farrar Straus Giroux Books for Young Readers
175 Fifth Avenue, New York 10010

Color separations by Bright Arts (H.K.) Ltd.
Printed in China by Toppan Leefung Printing Ltd.,
Dongguan City, Guangdong Province
Designed by Kristie Radwilowicz
Previous editions published by Golden Books Publishing and Tractor Mac, LLC
First Farrar Straus Giroux edition, 2015
1 3 5 7 9 10 8 6 4 2

mackids.com

Library of Congress Cataloging-in-Publication Data
Steers, Billy, author, illustrator.
Tractor Mac learns to fly / Billy Steers. — First Farrar Straus Giroux edition.
pages cm
Originally published by Golden Books in 2000.
Summary: After seeing a plane flying through the sky, Mac the tractor decides that he wants to fly.
ISBN 978-0-374-30103-3 (paper over board)
[1. Tractors—Fiction. 2. Flight—Fiction. 3. Self-acceptance—Fiction.] I. Title.

PZ7.S81536Tr 2015
[E]—dc23

2014040396

Farrar Straus Giroux Books for Young Readers may be purchased for business or promotional use. For information on bulk purchases please contact Macmillan Corporate and Premium Sales Department at (800) 221-7945 x5442 or by email at specialmarkets@macmillan.com.

ABOUT THE AUTHOR

Billy Steers is an author, illustrator, and commercial pilot. In addition to the Tractor Mac series, he has worked on forty other children's books. Mr. Steers had horses and sheep on the farm where he grew up in Connecticut. Married with three sons, he still lives in Connecticut. Learn more about the Tractor Mac books at www.tractormac.com.

Tractor Mac™